BREAKOUT ON PUFFIN ISLAND

By

Mandy Imlay
Illustrated by Jacqueline Tee

Grosvenor House
Publishing Limited

This book is published by
Grosvenor House Publishing Ltd
Link House
140 The Broadway, Tolworth, Surrey, KT6 7HT.
www.grosvenorhousepublishing.co.uk

A CIP record for this book
is available from the British Library

ISBN 978-1-78623-459-9

DEDICATION

This book is dedicated to my three beautiful children, Sam, Tom and Charlotte and my special stepsister Katherine and step-niece Grace.

ACKNOWLEDGEMENTS

I want to thank my greatest teacher, the Holy Spirit. This is your work, thank you for allowing me to help you bring it to fruition.

Thank you, Jackie Tee, for bringing this story to life with your beautiful illustrations and for all your advice, I couldn't have done it without you.

Dr Howard Morgan, thank you for mentoring me from afar and teaching me not to take myself too seriously and to enjoy playing with the Holy Spirit.

Rosie Smith, thank you for all the time you invested in me and for teaching me about creativity and the importance of simplicity and childlikeness.

Wendy Bates, thank you for turning up at certain times of my life when I was stuck, the breakthrough always came after you left.

Rev Pam Gordon, thank you for teaching me about the healing power of Jesus.

Carin Rosen, thank you for helping me learn so much about healing and myself, for your friendship, encouragement and hospitality.

CONTENTS

FAMILY TREE

Archibald & Matilda

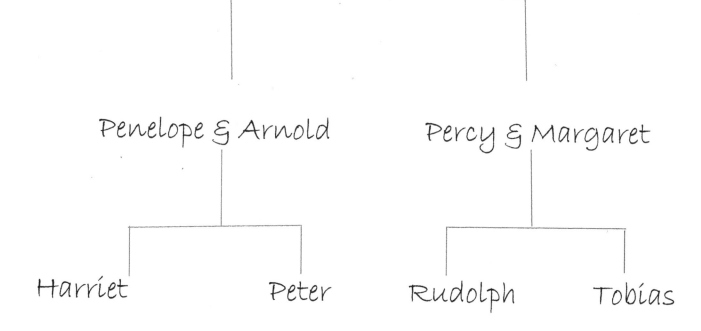

Penelope & Arnold

Percy & Margaret

Harriet

Peter

Rudolph

Tobias

CHAPTER 1

A RATHER SURPRISING DEVELOPMENT

Archibald Puffin was very tired, he had had a very busy day. As the patriarch puffin, Archibald, grandfather extraordinaire, had been listening to his children and grandchildren's problems all day long.

It's all very well being a referee but when can I go and have some fun? he thinks as he settles himself into his favourite rocking chair. He closes his eyes and remembers a time long ago when life seemed so simple and such a lot of fun. I don't seem to laugh much anymore Archibald realised with a jolt. When did life get so serious?

He was awoken by a tugging on his wing, "Grandfather, grandfather, wake up!" pipes up Peter Puffin.

Archibald brushes Peter off, but resigns himself to listen. Peter has a habit of going on and on and getting so over-excited that it is simpler to nod and agree with him, for only then will Archibald get his prized peace and quiet.

Unfortunately for grandfather Archibald, he didn't really listen at all. He nodded without paying proper attention and found himself agreeing with Peter before drifting off again into his well-deserved afternoon nap.

The next morning, there was much flapping and deep grunting coming from Puffin Island. All the puffins seemed to be in uproar and little Peter seemed to be beside himself, puffing out his little chest with importance. It was his time, grandfather had agreed, it was time for him to fly further than any of his brothers and sisters, he was going to fly to Sweden. He had often heard grandfather talk of his days in Sweden and all the many adventures he had had, and now, he too, was to be allowed to fly further than anyone else, and the best thing of all was that grandfather had agreed to come too!

CHAPTER 2

BREAKFAST RUINED!

Matilda Puffin barged into Archibald's bedroom with his usual morning cocktail of fish. She was banging about in a most unusual way, normally his beautiful wife was so loving and gentle. He opened one eye and looked and then the other eye was forced to follow suit.

"Whatever is the matter, Beloved?" he asks stretching out his bright orange feet. His webbed toes begin their usual exercise routine to encourage his circulation and help remove the stiffness in his joints.

"What's the matter? What's the matter indeed! I thought I knew you, I thought we discussed everything and here you are going off on your travels with Peter without a care in the world for me. And how you think you can fly all the way to Sweden beats me. Quite ridiculous ... quite ridiculous!"

Archibald began to choke on his fish, which did happen from time to time. Matilda went into action banging her wing over his back with great force. The fish was propelled out of Archibald's mouth and landed on the floor beside him. With extreme courage the little fish jumps for freedom, slithering off the rock and falling through the air and back into the welcoming arms of the blue sea below.

"Stop it Puffy!" Archibald managed to shout as Matilda's onslaught came to an end. Matilda looked shocked and began to sob uncontrollably. Archibald was a little uncomfortable, he never knew what to do with all this emotion, but he reached out towards her and after a while she came and huddled up for a cuddle. Archibald Puffin began to see what had happened.

"It is all a misunderstanding, Beloved, I am not going anywhere. It's that young Peter and his flights of imagination. I will go and sort it out! Help me up, will you?"

he says as he struggles to bring his feet under his body. Relief floods over Matilda Puffin as she hands him his walking stick.

"You can't go out like that, Archie. Look at the state of your bill!"
Archibald catches a glimpse of his reflection in a puddle and sees the muck still hanging onto his beak after the battle for his breakfast. He reaches over and washes himself in the puddle and heads down towards the waiting colony, fear suddenly wrapping itself around his belly like a tight belt.

"Oh dear," he thinks, "I must learn to listen more carefully."

CHAPTER 3

THE COLONY ASSEMBLES

Archibald makes his way down the rock, waddling awkwardly onto the slightly raised platform where he stood to address the colony. Everyone was there, waiting expectantly. There was a palpable feeling of excitement running through the now very depleted colony.

Peter was in the front row and was dancing with excitement, his little feet tapping out a tune, a beat that was beginning to get into Archibald's head. An irritating little tune that would not be ignored, every time he went to sweep it away and give his usual dampening down speech, it jolted him awake again. He looked out over his family and saw that many of the youngsters had shining eyes, the usual dullness had been replaced. He looked over at the older ones and saw what was reflected in his own belly, raw fear!

The little tune began to sing a song, it's voice knocking persistently in Archibald's head.

It is time to play,
It is time to fly,
No more fear,
No more fear.
The world awaits,
More adventures,
More songs.
It is time to play,
It is time to fly.

Grandfather Puffin opens his mouth and begins to sing the song he is hearing.

It is time to play,
It is time to fly,
No more fear,
No more fear.
The world awaits,
More adventures,
More songs.
It is time to play,
It is time to fly.

A stunned silence! Grandfather never sings! A ripple of unrest begins to move through the puffins and ever so gradually Archibald sees his dear ones separate out into two distinct camps, the ones in favour of change and the ones resistant to it.

What was so surprising was that many of the older ones had joined Peter's camp, including his very own Matilda. The other camp was headed up by grumpy Graham and many of the old guard, but also surprisingly many of the youngsters. These youngsters were always the ones with very little imagination, the ones who followed all the rules without question, the boring ones Archibald caught himself thinking in surprise.

"Goodness me," he thinks, "I have become very boring myself over these last few years. Boring and safe, not wanting to step out of my comfort zone, not wanting to rock the boat."

He retreats quietly into the background and walks over to his special place, the rock overlooking the mainland in the distance. I haven't been here for a very long time, Archibald realises. When did I stop dreaming? He wanders with a sigh.

He remembers when he first met Matilda, he was quite a catch then, a real adventurer. He was very like Peter, full of excitement, full of dreams. Oh how they had planned, they were going to travel to faraway places, they were going to learn how to stop the puffin pestilence, that great sickness that had been attacking the colonies for years. What had happened? How did we get so boxed in and dull?

CHAPTER 4

THE FIRST AID KIT

"Can I join you, Archie?" Matilda asks as he moves over to accommodate her rather ample bottom. Archibald had always loved Matilda's bottom, he had always celebrated it, he could never understand how the skinny squadron could be remotely attractive. What was the point of not eating the wonderful fish provided so abundantly for us? It made no sense to him at all. Most of the skinny squadron had joined grumpy Graham, Archibald realised, all of a sudden. Interesting, there might be something in this?

Matilda began to speak. "I am so proud of you, Archie, I know I was resisting at first, but when you sang that beautiful song something changed inside me, I was blind but now I see. This is who you are, this is who I married, I am so glad you have come back!"

Archie, choked back the tears that suddenly came from nowhere, and yet, they would not be kept at bay. At last he gave in and began to sob as if he would never be able to stop. They huddled together on that rock, an emotion deeper than either of them really understood surrounded them like a blanket and kept them both warm from the cold wind blowing from the north.

Time passed as they held one another and let the silence fill the space in their minds that was normally filled up with the mundane, the ordinary things in life. It is surprising the thoughts we have when we make space, thinks Archie. It's as if a whole new area of my brain has jumped to attention, bringing with it some very revolutionary ideas.

"So what if we did go to Sweden with Peter?"

"What me too?" Matilda managed to squeak suddenly feeling incredibly weak. Normally so capable, this seemed to have totally floored his beloved.

"Well, of course, I am not going without you, you are part of me, I cannot function without you. After all, who would bash me on the back when I get my coughing fits?" he laughed.

Matilda looked shyly up at him through her lashes and said, "But I am female, it is not allowed!"

"Oh stuff and nonsense, who made that rule up? If I am going so are you!"

As Archie looked over at Matilda, he was amazed to see the young puffin he had married suddenly appear, a sense of joy poured out from among her feathers and he realised sadly how he had contributed to her unhappiness.

''Puffins unite!" he said gruffly, the emotion surprising him so much that he fell flat on his face.

"Aw!" he squawked and Matilda came to the rescue with her first aid kit, that beautiful bill tapping away all the hurt.

CHAPTER 5

THE LIGHTHOUSE

There was a lot of organising to be done, now the decision to go had been made. They met with all the colony in groups and explained their decision. There appeared to be two sorts of reaction, either huge laughter and disbelief or admiration and support. Graham's gang could not believe what was happening and kept telling them that they would never succeed, their health would deteriorate even further and the journey might even kill them!

Very encouraging, chuckled Archibald to himself, but nothing could dampen his spirits. He hadn't felt so alive in years and he had positively jumped out of bed that morning, no exercises, no gentle coming to, no breakfast in bed and the miracle was no stiffness, no aching in his joints. In fact, he hadn't used his stick since that day on the rock when he and Matilda had decided to get radical and go after the adventure.

Peter and his gang had been amazing. They kept telling their grandparents that they were puffin changers, that they could do this and gradually Matilda and Archie had begun to believe it was true. They had handed all their duties over to others, who seemed to be honoured to be asked. They had taken over extremely well, so well in fact, that Archie realised he should have let go and passed over the baton of leadership a long time ago. New changes were afoot, new puffins, new life. But the odd thing was that Archie didn't feel remotely rejected, but instead felt free for the very first time to be the puffin he was always meant to be. He had been made to fly and have adventures whereas puffin Paul had risen into the leadership role effortlessly and had already made changes for the better. Everyone seemed happier, even grumpy Graham grudgingly approved the changes.

In a matter of just four weeks, they were ready, their expedition team was to be made up of themselves, Penelope their daughter and her husband Arnold, their son Peter and the twins, Rudolph and Tobias. The twins were Peter's cousins and they were inseparable.

Matilda had been in charge of supplies for the journey. The amount of stuff she had collected was quite extraordinary. Archie knew he would have to tell

13

her soon that they could take nothing with them. It would weigh them down and they would never get to Swedish shores carrying all that baggage.

It was time to visit the lighthouse one last time before they left. He knew all they needed would be found there. They would be given instructions where to fly to and the right direction to take. Archibald Puffin rounded up his troops and all seven of them headed off to the lighthouse.

Peter was intrigued. "Why do we need to go to the lighthouse, grandfather?

"Come and see!" grandfather said excitedly grabbing Peter's wing, and off they all went flying towards it's high tower.

Once they had all arrived safely at the top, William, the wise old owl appeared, as Archie had known he would.

Archie and Matilda knew William well, although they had neglected him of late. Penelope and Arnold had met William before, but only a handful of times, however, this was the first time the youngsters had met the wise old owl.

"Shouldn't you be asleep?" asked the ever inquisitive Peter looking at William.

"Oh, it's far too light and hot up here to sleep," hooted the great brown owl.

"I am no ordinary owl, in fact, I am completely opposite to what you puffins think. I never sleep!" William finished off winking widely at Archie and Matilda. They chuckled as they watched Peter and the others look dumbfounded.

"But owls always sleep during the day ..." trailed off Peter uncertainly.

"Yes, well that has always been the perception, but things are not always what you think," continued William gently.

"Right, it is time for some flying exercises," William said, pointing out to sea with his wing.

"But we know how to fly!" said Peter and the twins together.

"Do you?"

"Of course we do, we are puffins aren't we!" said Peter.

"Well, let's see, shall we," said William gently.

"Right, first of all you, Archibald and Matilda. I want you to fly across to that little island over there in the distance. When you get there, I want you to rest. Look around you and you will find plenty to eat and drink. Enjoy your time there and take time to notice the signs I have left there for you."

"Ok!" they both replied in unison and off they waddled to the side of the lighthouse and launched themselves out towards the horizon.

William then turns to Penelope and Arnold and repeats the same thing and off they go excitedly in the same direction.

William turns to the youngsters, but before William can get anything out of his mouth, Peter pipes up, "I know, I know what to do, come on Toby and Rudy, let's go!" and off the three of them go flying high into the sky.

CHAPTER 6

UNDER THE APPLE TREE

Archie and Matilda arrive at last at the little island. They are tired and out of breath and gladly lie down next to the still calm water of the little lake covering the bottom part of the island in the shade of the old apple tree. It is very warm but the branches reach out like a canopy covering them completely.

"The leaves are very green aren't they Archie," remarks Matilda as she begins to breathe more easily.

"They certainly are, my love, much greener than on Puffin Island."

They drink deeply of the clear refreshing water and lie down to rest. They drift off to sleep with a satisfied contentment that comes after exercise and fresh air. How I have missed this, thinks Archie before he drifts off to sleep.

Sometime later, they wake up to the sound of splashing. As they look out over the lake, they see a sight that is quite startling. Matilda rubs her eyes and looks again.

"Am I dreaming or are those fish just jumping out of the lake and lying there for us to eat?"

Archie begins to laugh and says, "So it seems, how very fortunate we are. No fishing seems necessary, how very easy!"

He reaches out and brings the fish over to Matilda and they share the most wonderful meal together.

After a little while, Archie says, "I am going in for a swim," and off he goes.

After Matilda had recovered from the shock of seeing her ailing husband swimming with abandon in the lake, she jumps in to join him, laughing hilariously. Everything seems so funny all of a sudden and all the tiredness and pain in her knees just disappears.

"There is something very special about this place," remarks Matilda and Archie just nods, as such a feeling of wellbeing and happiness comes over him.

The puffins begin to frolic and play together like youngsters, just enjoying one another and everything provided for them.

CHAPTER 7

THE SONG AND THE EAGLE

On another part of the island, Arnold and Penelope have arrived. They find themselves at a beautiful crystal clear lake and drink their fill, letting the deliciously cool water drop down their throats and wash their beautiful orange bills quite clean.

Something very strange begins to happen. They start to sing, both so in tune with one another that it is impossible to know where one voice begins and the other ends. All they know is that this song soared up inside them both, it was a song of love, it was a song of joy.

"Let's go fishing!" shouts Arnold as he dives into the water having spied his favourite fish. Penelope was not going to be left behind and in they both go. After a while they catch enough to eat and sit down contentedly to enjoy the feast. After they had eaten, they thought they had better start looking for those signs that William had left for them. They searched and searched until it got too dark to see any further, so they nestled up together, glad of one another's feathers to keep them warm as they slept.

Meanwhile, the cold north wind had begun to blow and the three young puffins were being blown off course. Peter was flying energetically out in front, he knew just where he was headed. At one point, Rudolph came to take the lead pointing a little further to the left, but no, Peter knew better and after a brief tussle the twins bowed to Peter's obviously superior navigational skills and followed his lead.

Time passed and darkness began to fall. Despite all his bravado, Peter was beginning to feel a little uneasy and very tired.

"We must have lost our way a little," he admitted when the twins were brave enough to challenge him.

"We must rest, Peter, I can't fly much further," Tobias managed to say breathlessly. The three youngsters were beginning to feel very frightened indeed.

Overhead, a large shadow passed over them, only it wasn't a shadow, they discovered, but an enormous bird with a wide wing on each side. It swooped gracefully underneath the three puffins and spoke in a surprisingly, gentle but deep voice.

"Would you like some help, my little friends?"

Peter was about to proudly refuse when he saw the look the twins gave him and so he reluctantly said yes and then added please as he remembered what his mother kept telling him.

The great eagle put out its wing and the three puffins climbed on board, they made a very weary and dejected crew.

"Hold tight," said the eagle and swooped down and then up again, twisting and turning in summersaults in the air. The twins loved it, shouting out for more, but Peter it seems, was so overcome with motion sickness that he was completely unable to enjoy the rest of the journey.

CHAPTER 8

THE HEAVENLY CHOIR

The sun begins to rise and the birds begin to stir, raising their voices in a beautiful dawn chorus. Archie and Matilda wake up to the sweetest concert. They decide to get to know the birds that make up this glorious choir.

There were the beautiful yellow canaries who were the sopranos, they sang higher and higher than it seemed possible to sing.

There were the blue tits with their alto harmonies joining their friends. The altos sang a bit lower than the canaries and helped to keep perfect balance. Looking out further into the distance, they saw the red breasted robins trilling out powerfully in their deep and yet at the same time high notes. A deep bass beat drummed out from behind the other birds. There at the back sat William and his like, bringing the whole song together with their deep cooing.

The owls seemed so sleepy and yet Archie was aware that without these bass notes, the choir was unfinished and seemingly without an anchor. An understanding began to fill Archie's mind, he turned to Matilda and saw the same knowing look appear over her dear face.

"Why, we need William, we cannot do anything without his wise words and his direction!" splutters Matilda in surprise.

William winks at them and points to one of the yellow canaries. Round its neck is tied a note, Matilda reaches out and takes it and hands it to Archie to read.

"You read it," says Archie unwilling to admit that he had come without his glasses. Matilda squints and then admits that she too had forgotten her glasses. Suddenly, William appears with a magnifying glass and together they read the note.

"WELCOME TO THE YACHT CLUB!"

How extraordinary they both think, what does it mean? Meanwhile, William points to a blue tit who is sitting with its head to one side looking inquisitively up at the puffins. Underneath her little foot is a piece of blue material with embroidery over the front of it. She waits until the puffins notice her and then kicks it over towards them. They pick it up together, marvelling at all the intricate and beautiful colours sewn into the picture.

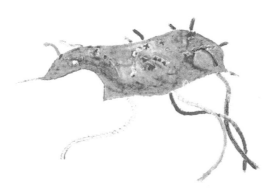

"Well, what is it?" asks Archie.

The blue tit turns it over and underneath the puffins see all the hard work and wrong turns that have been made to bring this beautiful picture together.

"What is the picture, William?" asks Matilda.

"It is the story of your lives," he answers, then he points to the red robin who has been sitting next to Archie and Matilda all this time, but they have only just noticed him.

He begins to sing a beautiful and yet sad song, but he sings in a language they have never heard before and so they still do not understand. William then hands them a key and points them in the direction of a little wooden cabin in the distance.

"How exciting!" says Matilda and follows Archie as he marches purposefully across to the cabin. They unlock the door and walk through. To their utter amazement, they seemed to have arrived in Sweden. Archie knows it is Sweden because he has been here before. This is the colony belonging to his cousin Sven.

CHAPTER 9

A SURPRISING NEW FRIEND

The rain began to pour down on Arnold and Penelope Puffin awakening them to a brand new day. They could see the dark clouds gathering in the distance and wondered if a storm was brewing. Going fishing for breakfast didn't seem at all inviting, nor did anything else for that matter. Hiding under the shelter of a large rock is what they normally did in bad weather, but they were on a quest to find signs so that they could return home and qualify to go to Sweden. Arnold and Penelope felt rather discouraged to say the least. They decided to move out and have a look around, which they did rather half-heartedly for quite some time.

"I am hungry, Arnie, and very tired," grumbled Penelope. Both puffins were really fed up and frustrated. They began to bicker and squabble with one another. Arnold had had enough and walked off to get some space.

After some time had passed and Arnold had not returned, Penelope began to worry. She decided that she had better try to find him or at least one of those elusive signs. She began to walk and took a narrow path leading through some trees. It was nice and warm here, sheltered from the wind and rain. As she went she ate some of the berries on the trees and although they weren't fish, she rather liked their sweet taste.

A squirrel jumped from out of nowhere startling her. He had a hoard of nuts, some he was storing away for the winter, others he was busily enjoying.

"Hello!" said Penelope in what she hoped was a friendly manner. She had heard stories of squirrels and knew they could be tricky customers. This squirrel wasn't one of the large grey ones she had heard about, it was smaller and reddish in colour with a very bushy tail.

"Hello yourself. You are lost!" he pronounced with confidence.

Well really, thought Penelope, isn't that rather obvious, but not wanting to offend, she smiled readily and agreed that she was indeed lost and needed help.

"I am Stuart," said the squirrel throwing her a nut. "I expect you are hungry."

Puffins don't normally eat nuts and Penelope was rather at a loss at how to proceed. Stuart, seeing her predicament removed the outer hard layer for her and she bit into the nut. As she did a funny feeling began to come over her. Tears sprang into her eyes and she felt an alarming affection for the squirrel in front of her. How weird, she thought, to feel love for someone I have only just met.

"Follow me, Penny," said Stuart and so she did. After a little while, she suddenly realised that she hadn't told him her name.

"How did you know ..." she began, when Stuart interrupted her.

"I was told to expect you!"

Penelope was surprised.

"William!" Stuart explained and ran off into the forest. She began to fly in a haphazard way trying to avoid the many overhanging branches. After some time had passed, they arrived at a clearing.

"Wait here," he said and scampered off once more.

She looked around and saw a little stream and began to drink thirstily. Then she sat down under an enormous apple tree and fell fast asleep.

CHAPTER 10

REUNITED AT LAST

Meanwhile, Arnold had calmed down and thought he had better return to rescue Penelope. He was very wet, cold and hungry. However, when he returned to find her, Penelope was nowhere to be seen.

Arnold was rather alarmed calling out, "Penny, Penny," over and over, squawking louder and louder and getting himself into a real panic. He began to hyperventilate until he was convinced he was having a heart attack.

"Can I help you, sir?" croaked a little frog sitting a little to his left.

Arnold was rather put out, what good will a frog be, he needed a doctor not a frog, he thought dismissively. However, after a while his chest was hurting so much, he nodded.

The little frog jumped up onto Arnold's chest and began to croak.

Oh for goodness sake thought Arnold in extreme irritation, but all of a sudden the pain stopped and he felt a calmness pour all over him.

The little frog smiled up at Arnold and introduced herself as Frieda.

"How did you do that?" asked Arnold in surprise.

"Oh, it's all about who you know," Frieda replied.

"Oh and by the way, the other puffin went that way," she said pointing towards the forest.

"Thank you so much, you have been incredibly helpful," said Arnold, "and I am so sorry that I judged you and dismissed you as unimportant. I was wrong and I am very sorry."

Frieda nodded and smiled, "I was glad that I could help you, goodbye, Arnie."

Arnold was half way through the forest before he realised that he hadn't told Frieda his name. A very different Arnold arrived at the clearing, and when he saw his Penny, he was delighted and ran over to embrace her.

Oh, how they had missed one another, they had both had quite a scare, but they were determined to stick together in future. They drank some more from the stream and miraculously saw some fish hiding just under a rock. Arnie dived in and caught one for Penny and one for himself. They enjoyed a delicious meal under the apple tree and then cuddled up together to wait for what would happen next.

CHAPTER 11

THE CROSSROADS

The great eagle landed on a rock at the top of the little island. He turned to the youngsters and said, "Now, my friends, it is time for you to make your own way. Follow that road until you get to a crossroads, turn left and keep going until you come to a lake. There you will find all you need."

They thanked the eagle and began to walk along the road.

"Don't forget to follow my directions, turn left at the crossroads!" he called after them and flew higher and higher until they could see him no longer.

Daylight was breaking and the sun was beginning to rise and there was a gentle golden glow covering the sky. They arrived at last at the crossroads where the sign pointed left to the lake and right to the restaurant.

"Oh, let's go to the restaurant first, I'm starving" said Peter.

"No, no, no!" chimed the twins in unison. "This time we are going to listen and follow the directions. The eagle even reminded us just as he flew off."

Of course, they were absolutely right realised Peter sadly. We all have choices to make, but so often we choose the wrong way because we take our eyes off our destination. I have been easily distracted in the past thought Peter with a shock. He decided to let the twins lead for a change.

They arrived at the lake as the sun shone high in the sky. Three little puffins looking rather worse for wear! They dived into the lake and drank and drank. The water seemed to revive and refresh the weary travellers and they began to search for some fish. After a little while Toby shouted out, he had found a lovely rainbow trout hiding in the shallows. Rudy and Peter followed him as he chased the trout round and round and round again.

"It's no good, Rudy and Toby," says Peter at last. He suddenly knows what they should do. Nothing! The wise old owl had told them to rest and to be honest, he was exhausted, he felt he couldn't do any more. They huddled together under the apple tree and fell fast asleep.

"Quack, quack, quack, quack!" A great orange bill appeared and pushed them rudely out from under the tree.

"How long have you been here? I was expecting you three yesterday, what kept you?

"It's a long story," said Rudy.

"But we are here now," said Toby excitedly.

"So I see!" said the duck looking at the three puffins closely.

"Well, I expect you are hungry, you had better follow me."

They followed the duck to the other side of the lake, where there were plenty of fish to choose from. When they had eaten their fill, they turned once more to the duck.

"Why do you have a stopwatch around your neck?" asked Peter, noticing it for the first time.

"My name is Gloria, by the way and it is time for TIME OUT!" she picked up the stopwatch and pressed down the button and the clock stopped.
"Now, you have to wait, rest and enjoy yourselves. Wait and keep your eyes open," and off she went flying into the air with a huge ruffle of feathers.

This time the puffins did as they were told. Suddenly all their energy seemed to disappear and they just sat together talking and sleeping for what seemed a very long time. Days passed and the three young puffins lost all track of time. Everything they needed was right there by the lake and under the shade of the apple tree. They got to know each other like never before and they started to notice the beauty of the world around them, simple pleasures provided abundantly for them to enjoy.

"I wonder why we have never noticed these things before?" said Rudy.
"Because we were always too busy," said Peter, "too busy to see what was right under our beaks!"

34

CHAPTER 12

THE SNOWBALL FIGHT

In Sweden, it had begun to snow, much to Archie and Matilda's delight, they hadn't seen snow for a very long time. They had forgotten how beautiful everything looked covered in a blanket of white fluffiness. Now, instead of being afraid that they would slip and fall, the puffins began to have a snowball fight. They were having a lot of fun when suddenly out of nowhere came hurtling a very thick snowball from a completely different direction. The snowball caught them both off guard and sent them into a frenzied heap with feathers and legs flying everywhere. Severely winded, they both sat rather dazed on their bottoms in the snow.

"Who are you and what are you doing here? This is private property and you are trespassing!" announced the stranger haughtily. They looked up to see a very tall bird towering down over them, it's legs seemed to go on and on forever. Archie struggled to his feet and helped Matilda up. He explained that he was Sven's cousin and that they had come for a visit. The bird looked them over with her beady eye and then flew off.

"Well, how rude!" said Matilda rather shocked, suddenly feeling very unsure of herself. What should we do Archie?"

"I think it would be a good idea to make our way to the island and find Sven and then everything will be sorted out," he said with more confidence than he felt and so they took the road which Archie remembered. The snow which had previously given them so much joy suddenly became rather foreboding and cold.

After what seemed a very long time, although in truth was probably only half a mile, they arrived at the lake where they would find Sven's boat. He always kept a little boat on both sides of the lake in case of unexpected visitors. The light was fading fast and Archie saw that the boat would be no use at all, as the lake was completely frozen.

Out from the undergrowth appeared a beaver bearing skates.

"Hello, I am Theodore and William has sent me. You are going to have to learn to use these," he smiles holding out the skates towards the two astounded puffins.

"But we can't skate!" screeched Matilda, fear rising up from her belly and out of her mouth.

"Well, you are going to have to learn!" said Theodore and began to show them how to put the skates on. Skates were obviously not made for puffins and their little webbed feet kept falling out of the little skate shoes.

"I think we are going to need some help," said the beaver and disappeared into the undergrowth once more. He returned with some string and began to tie parts of the skate shoe to their feet. After a while, he seemed satisfied and told them to stand up and hang onto him until they found their balance.

"Well, this is going to be interesting," said Archie fully expecting to fall flat on his face. Theodore stared at Archie and told him to focus on his eyes. Incredibly as Archie did just that, he was able to not only stand up but began to skate confidently onto the ice.

"Come on, Mattie, it's easy!" he shouts, but as he glances over towards Matilda, he loses his balance and comes crashing down hard.

Matilda winced, knowing how much that would have hurt Archie's pride as well as his bottom! No one likes to fail and Archie had always been a very proud puffin, shying away from anything that he felt he couldn't succeed at. As a result, of course, he had not done very much at all. Theodore picked Archie up effortlessly and told him to keep his eyes on him. He must not be distracted by anyone or anything else.

"I will come back for Matilda after you are safely across," the beaver says and off they go once more.

Ten exhilarating minutes later, Archie arrives at the other side and waves back at Matilda encouragingly. Theodore returns and helps Matilda to do the same thing. She kept her eyes on his, in fact she found it very hard to look away, so mesmerising were those soft brown eyes. In no time at all, Matilda too, reached the island and they gratefully thanked the beaver for all his help.

"No problem," he said and handed them some string to carry their skates.

"You will find Sven and the colony up at the north side of that rock," he said and off he went back to the other side of the lake.

CHAPTER 13

SHOOTING STARS

Although darkness had fallen and it was very cold, there was a bright full moon and the sky was crystal clear. They could see a startling display of lights, with sparkling stars shooting out across the night sky. The puffins were mesmerised by the beauty and majesty of it all and just watched for some time.

"Well, I suppose we had better make a start," said Archie reluctantly.

"Yes, I suppose so," agreed Matilda.

"Do you know, Archie, I think William has arranged this whole display of light just for us. It was completely dark on the other side of the lake."
"Yes, I think you are absolutely right. There is more to William than we realised."

The puffins began to fly across to the northern rock as Theodore had directed them. Their wings seemed strangely light and despite carrying their skates, they were thoroughly enjoying the journey.
In the distance, the tall foreboding stranger returned and Matilda realised that it was a stork. Another stork accompanied it and they both encircled Archie and Matilda. Although they didn't speak, now it seemed as if they were friendly and they guided them gently to a large rock.

Waiting for them was Sven and his shy wife Hanne. Behind them crowded a huge colony of puffins awaiting their arrival excitedly. Archie and Matilda were completely overcome by the welcome they received, they felt like royalty. They were given the most wonderful fish supper followed by the best place to sleep. The view from their nesting place was quite spectacular and overlooked the sea in the distance. They fell asleep contentedly together, still digesting the enormity of what had just happened. Just before she drifted off into dreamland, Matilda realised that Archie had not coughed or choked on his fish once since they had left home. She snuggled up under his wing happily, listening to his gentle snoring in the background.

CHAPTER 14

THE DOVE'S SONG AND THE TOXIC CLOUD

41

Back on the island, soot filled the air and ash began to rain down from the sky over Arnold and Penelope. They breathed in the contaminated air and they began to cough and splutter. A dark cloud suddenly hovered directly over the two puffins and they began to find it increasingly difficult to breathe.

"What is happening?" Penelope asked a rather bewildered Arnold, who just shook his head and concentrated on his breathing. Panic began to set in once more and the two puffins were very scared, very scared indeed.

"We need to find William," Penelope managed to squeak and as soon as she did, out of the corner of her eye she saw the two large storks. They picked up the dark toxic cloud in their beaks and began to move it out of the way. Their breathing became easier as the air became clean once more. The panic disappeared and the peace returned as a pretty pink coloured cloud surrounded the puffins and a supernatural protection was put in place.

A wonderful scent filled the air and they began to hear a beautiful song. They looked out over the lake to where there was a pure white dove and she was singing the most beautiful song they had ever heard.

Suddenly, and quite unexpectedly Arnie grabbed Penelope in his wings and said, "let's dance!"

She was so surprised at this turn of events that she was drawn along with her powerful puffin of a husband and they whirled and twirled delightedly for what seemed like hours. So lost in the beauty of the song were they that they

were astounded to discover that they had been dancing all day without even thinking about food.

The song had now ended, however, and miraculously there on the grass sat a feast of fish for the puffins to eat.

"How amazing, how wonderful!" they exclaimed together and began to feed greedily on the most delicious fish they had ever tasted.

Penelope suddenly blurted out, "Why Arnie, I never knew you could be so romantic!"

"Neither did I," admitted Arnold feeling ever so handsome and attractive all of a sudden. A knowing confidence came over him and he knew who he was. He was an adventurer and a pioneer, he was creative and handsome. How startling, he thought, that he had never realised that before. He had always been kept down by others and rather passed over. Except by his Penny, of course, she had always known that he had strength and potential, but he hadn't believed her. How very extraordinary, he could see everything so clearly all of a sudden.

Happily, they huddled up together, watching the stars in the night sky and gradually the puffins fell asleep. Hovering overhead was a beautiful golden eagle keeping watch over these precious puffins. Nothing would get past him!

CHAPTER 15

THE POOL AND A WHOLE NEW UNDERWATER WORLD

It started to rain, gently at first and then more heavily. The three young puffins retreated to the shelter of the apple tree. The drops began to dance on the green leaves, falling into a pool which began to form at their feet. The pool seemed to grow bigger and bigger by the minute and a beautiful light glowed out from its middle. As they looked, the light began to become more distinct and they could see a beautiful rainbow emerge from out of the pool and reach up into the sky beyond.

"Wow!" said Peter breathlessly, and the twins just nodded in agreement, too overcome to put what they were seeing into words.

There was an almighty splash and out of the pool jumped a large blue dolphin. It began to summersault playfully, waving its tail in the air. The next minute two seals had joined the dolphin and a ball materialized out of thin air. The pool had become very large by this time and the puffins jumped in to join in this exciting game of water ball. There were certain rules to follow it seemed, and yet not like the rules and regulations of the past. There was a fluidity about it, nothing was rigid and yet there was a gentle pattern emerging holding the whole game together.

Underneath the water, Peter and the twins realised there was a very large octopus with its eight long tentacles trying to trap the ball and stop the game. The dolphin and the seals were very clever and seemed to foil the octopus' plan at every stage. The octopus was getting grumpier and grumpier with every minute.

"Oh, I have had enough of this!" said the dolphin and handed Peter, Rudy and Toby a sword each. After they had recovered from the shock of three swords appearing out of thin air, the puffins looked back at the dolphin for further instructions.

The dolphin introduced himself as Daniel and then proceeded to use his own, larger sword to knight the three puffins by bringing the blade down to rest gently on each of their heads.

"Arise, my brave warriors, you are three musketeers and you will go forth and perform exploits for our King!" said Daniel grandly.

The puffins were completely lost for words, everything was getting weirder and weirder and yet, this was the most exciting time they had ever had!

"Who is our King?" asked the ever inquisitive Peter.

"Well, William Owl, of course, he is the King of this whole Kingdom," honked the seals in unison. Understanding came at last, as the three young puffins could see what had been in front of their eyes all along.

"Oh dear," said Rudy, "we haven't respected and honoured William, we didn't realise who he was."

They all looked rather dejected and shamefaced.

"You can tell him you are sorry to his face, here he comes!" said Daniel flipping upside down and diving down into the depths of the pool again, the seals followed suit and the pool became as still as a pond once more.

A big owl arrived hooting into the night sky. The darkness had fallen and yet this owl was snowy white and radiated light, not brown and small like William at all. The three puffins bowed low before this majestic, awesome owl, they could do nothing but lie at his feet. After a while, they heard William's gentle but deep voice speaking to them in that familiar kind tone that they recognised. They looked up and there was William, all brown and quite ordinary looking really.

The puffins were too surprised to speak and so William kindly began to explain.

"You just caught a glimpse of my heavenly form, but this would be too much for you to cope with normally, so I choose to appear to you in a more ordinary way. I had to show you the truth, so that you would listen to me and follow my ways. For I know the best for you, because I can see the bigger picture, whereas, you can only see the situation you are in. Now, are you three willing to follow me and perform exploits and help set the rest of the puffins free?"

"Oh, yes please," they all replied at once, and so William continued.

"It is time to pick up your swords and to dive down under the water. Daniel and the seals, Dotty and Duncan will help you. You are to cut off every one of the octopus' eight tentacles, for he is guarding a cave full of puffins. Puffins who everyone thought were drowned and dead, but all the time they have been captured by the cruel Colin. Colin rules the underwater world and uses the octopus and many others to help him. But, you must remember that they are all his victims too. They have all been hurt and rejected and so they have set up

47

their own gangs here under the water. As you cut off each one of the octopus' arms and legs, you will see him transform and become Oliver, the Mighty. He has been misled, he doesn't know who he is. I am sending you to show him the truth and help set him free. He will be one of my greatest supporters and he will rescue many, many others from every part of the underwater world."

"Wow," says Peter, his usual enthusiasm overcoming any caution.

"But Peter," William continues kindly, "you will all have to obey my instructions and do only what I show you to do. Anytime you do not hear directly from me or my trusted friends, then you are to wait and rest and keep doing what I have already told you to do. Is that clear?"

The three puffins agreed wholeheartedly, and as they did, the most extraordinary thing happened. Their hearts suddenly got bigger expanding out of their little chests and filling up the rest of their bodies, it was as if they had become completely see through and a very large beating heart inside each of their little bodies was the only thing to be seen.

CHAPTER 16

THE ORCHESTRA BEGINS TO COME TOGETHER

The owls were having a party in a very deep part of the forest. Not many creatures ventured this far, but those who did were richly rewarded. William was sitting on a large golden throne with a beautiful jewel encrusted crown on his head, next to him was his father and mother, Papa and Mama Owl, also with beautiful crowns on their heads. All three were watching a thrilling dance take place in a figure of eight, and all sorts of creatures were taking part. Each bird was leading a different group of instruments and all were coming together to bring about this beautiful symphony. There had been a few hiccups along the way, the lead violins had needed a bit of a kick to get them going, but now they were leading their sections with confidence. In each group every sort of instrument was represented, a string section, a brass and woodwind section as well as the exciting drums and cymbals.

As the different creatures played their given part, the most beautiful sound emerged, a sound which transported everyone who played into the very presence of William and his parents deep in the forest.

As they watched, more and more creatures began to arrive, seemingly out of nowhere. They all began to harmonize and join with one another in a beautiful symphony of togetherness.

The dancers were moving from the figure of eight and were beginning to draw a new number, the number 16. Such was the freedom and creativity displayed that William and his parents were in tears.

"This is what we have always dreamed of!" they hooted to one another, "this is just the beginning, those brave forerunners are going out to show the others the way."

The owls looked fondly out over the proceedings.

"These are our most special set apart ones, the trailblazers," they hooted and they began to sing over all the creatures in front of them.

CHAPTER 17

DISCOVERING WHAT FREEDOM LOOKS LIKE

Morning had arrived in Sweden and Hanne went to rouse her guests. "Time to wake up, sleepy heads," she whispered hesitantly, bringing her guests their breakfast. The sun was high in the sky, how long had they been asleep they wondered? Matilda lay quietly trying to remember her dream while Archibald sprang into action, the army training of his past suddenly coming to the fore. Off he went energetically to wash in the pond and to straighten his feathers before pulling on his pants with enthusiasm.

"Well, what a transformation!" beamed Matilda gazing adoringly at her husband, "but could you be a little bit quieter please, I am trying to remember my dream and I just know it is important ..." she trailed off in her usual serene way.

"Oh sorry, darling heart," he puffed tapping his bill on hers.

"I am off for my early morning exercise," and off he flew up into the air showing off his newly found acrobatic prowess!

Matilda was rather amused and turned back reluctantly to try and remember her dream. But it was no good, it seemed to have run away from her on fast marching legs. Her thoughts returned to William and she wondered if he could help her remember her dream. I wonder where he is, she thought. Suddenly, a voice came out of nowhere.

"I am with you, dearest one," and there perched on the rock just outside their nesting place sat William.

Matilda was delighted, she had really missed William over the past few years. He used to visit her frequently when she was young, "I wonder when it stopped?" she asked herself.

"When you stopped believing!" William hooted knowingly.

Matilda looked shocked. "But I always believed!" she protested. Those soft green eyes bored into her own and she realised he was right.

"Oh I am so very sorry William," she managed quietly.

"It's ok sweetheart, I am just pleased you are back, I have missed you enormously, you are my special one."

Matilda was quite taken aback as she was wrapped in the most powerful wing hug she had ever experienced. She felt quite helpless, a weariness and heaviness came over her and she was completely undone. Time passed and eventually Matilda regained her composure and ruffled her feathers, patting down her rather unruly mop of tufts on her head. William smiled at her and began to speak.

"I have been speaking to you for years in your dreams, my love, because you were too busy to hear me while you were awake. The only time that I could get your attention was when you were flat out and unconscious!"

Matilda looked very shamefaced but William continued cheerfully, "but I will turn it all for the good. I want to take you to meet Papa and Mama Owl, they have been longing to meet you."

"Oh, how lovely," said Matilda Puffin and immediately jumped up on William's back.

"Hold on tight!" he said and off they went flying high into the air.

The higher they climbed, the heavier Matilda felt, that weakness was returning and she felt incapable of anything. She held on for dear life and stopped struggling. After some time, the heaviness lifted and a lightness and a joy came and took its place. Suddenly, she felt just like she used to when she was a little puffin and then her eyes began to see a picture. She rubbed them because she was not sure if she was imagining it or not, but the picture was still very much there.

Two little robin red breasts had come either side of her and they began to take off her brown apron. Well, really, she thought, they can't do that, but apparently they could. Matilda seemed to have lost her voice and the use of

54

her wings. The apron was removed and then they returned with a beautiful embroidered jumper in blues and greens and a golden scroll and a feather quill.

"The quill is for writing," explained the two robins and then they disappeared behind a cloud. Matilda was just getting her head around all this when William came in to land in the middle of a clearing in the forest.

They had arrived in a middle of a party, only it was a party like no other she had known. Puffins galore had congregated together and they appeared to be completely drunk … yes, there could be no other explanation for the great hilarity on display. Puffins were falling all over the place, laughing so hard that their bellies were hurting. Matilda was rather confused and impatient and looked around for William, but he seemed to have completely disappeared. She ruffled her feathers and was determined to show her displeasure at this disrespectful behaviour. She stood slightly aloof over towards the right of the clearing, wondering how she could escape.

She felt a tap on her wing and a puffin appeared in front of her. In surprise, she recognised the puffin as Marjorie, she had known her many years ago before she had married Archie. She had just disappeared one day and they all thought she had drowned or been eaten up.

"Marjorie, you are alive!" Matilda exclaimed in utter amazement.

"Yes, of course, I am," she replied.

"But where have you been?" Matilda continued in wonder.

"I have joined the Kingdom Army," she said, "and I live here now!"

Matilda was even more shocked.

"Oh poor you," she began, "you must come home with me, you cannot stay in this drunken madhouse!"

Marjorie laughed out loud, "but I love it here, it is the best thing that has ever happened to me. Life is never dull anymore, there are always adventures and exploits as well as lots of time to rest and enjoy ourselves".

Matilda was lost for words and she just did not understand. Marjorie reached over and poked her in the tummy and a spark ignited a flame inside her and the heat began to radiate up through Matilda Puffin in a most extraordinary way.

Bubbles of what she could only describe as pure joy began to pop out of her beak. The laughter began and she laughed and laughed, she cried and held her belly, she fell helpless on the floor and then she began to dance. She danced and danced, whirling and twirling with abandon. Oh, she felt so free, so uninhibited, so alive! She began to join in the party, enjoying every delicious moment. A thought came into her head, "I wish Archie was with me," and instantly there he was right in front of her, his eyes sparkling with delight and fun. They didn't need to communicate, Archibald Puffin, grandfather extraordinaire had had his own adventure, just as she had. Each adventure was tailor-made for each puffin to bring the healing they needed. They were both wearing their new blue and green embroidered jumpers!

"Oh, how wonderful is our William!" was all they could sing.

CHAPTER 18

DESTINIES REVEALED

What a wonderful banquet they had, as much fish as they could eat and plenty of water to drink. This water seemed very special indeed, it stopped them ever feeling thirsty again, it really was quite extraordinary. They met Papa and Mama Owl, they and William joined in the festivities with great gusto, embracing every puffin there and telling them that they were very special, and they really meant it!

After a while, the puffins retired to their own colonies and the clearing emptied. Archie and Matilda were left all alone with Papa and Mama Owl, even William seemed to have disappeared.

"Come over here," Papa said gently and patted the large red couch on which he was seated. Archie sat on one side and Matilda on the other. Mama waved goodbye and said she would be back later. Papa Owl reached out for each of their wings with his and held them firmly.

"It is time, my children for you to understand what we have planned for you, what your destiny is, what will bring you great joy."

A deep reverence and awe fell over the puffins simultaneously as they listened to Papa Owl. It seemed incredible that they should lead a new colony and live in Sweden, but this was what Papa Owl was wanting them to do. Not only that but Matilda was to become a writer and a teacher.

"New horizons await you both, my beloved children and we are so very pleased with you both."

Archie and Matilda were completely dumbfounded and were quite unable to comment one way or another.

Suddenly, Mama Owl appeared with an intoxicating cocktail full of colours and lovely smells. A whiff of haddock flew through the air and the two puffins drank deeply from the crystal clear glasses. As they finished, Mama Owl began

to go all funny, she became like a pinkish vapour and disappeared inside both Archie and Matilda. As Mama Owl entered inside the puffins, Archie and Matilda were given extraordinary courage and boldness and they suddenly began to speak in a foreign language.

Papa Owl was having great fun watching the two puffins, but at last he thought he had better explain.

"You two are highly favoured and have been called to Sweden to lead a new colony built on my special rock. Now you have been given the faith, power and the courage to do this, oh and by the way, the language you are speaking, is Swedish!

Remember, you are no more important than anyone else, all you did was say 'YES'. For, you are all special, the only qualification you need is to believe and receive everything we give you."

Mama Owl and William appeared again and they all came together for a group hug. A photograph was taken and was stuck into a large book on which was written; *THE ADVENTURES AND EXPLOITS OF ARCHIBALD AND MATILDA PUFFIN.*"

CHAPTER 19

DANCING SHOES

Arnold and Penelope awoke gradually to the feeling that they were no longer alone, and they weren't, for sitting on the edge of their nesting place on the island was William. He smiled kindly down on them with those beautiful green eyes of his. Those eyes always seemed to make the puffins melt and go all squishy inside.

"Have you been enjoying yourselves?" he asked and they both nodded and realised that they hadn't had such a romantic time since before their puffin brood had come along.

"I am so very glad," continued William, "for this is what you two puffins are called to do!"

Arnold and Penelope look rather shocked and so he began to explain.

"Not every puffin is called overseas, you know. Archibald and Matilda are called to Sweden, but just because they are, doesn't mean that you should do this too."

"Oh" said Arnold, "is that why we didn't find any signs?"

"Ah, but you did find signs, but just not the ones you were expecting! What has happened to you since you left home?"

Penelope said immediately, "We have fallen in love again and also we seem to love everyone we meet, even if they are total strangers!"

As Penelope finished speaking, Arnold realised that that was exactly what had happened to him as well, that little frog had really got under his skin!

William smiled and said, "Our work is nearly done," and there in front of the puffins, William separated out into three owls instead of one.

"Oh, this is Papa and Mama Owl," he said introducing them.

William's Papa and Mama seemed thrilled to be introduced, apparently they had been waiting a long time to make the puffins acquaintance.

How extraordinary thought Arnold, as if we are very important!

"You two are very special," said Papa Owl "and we have a very important mission for the two of you. We are sending you back home to your colony on Puffin Island because you are going to teach the other puffins all about love and how to dance that beautiful dance."

Penelope was suddenly so excited that she rushed over and threw herself onto Papa's lap reaching up for a big hug.

"That's exactly what I have always wanted to do!" she squawked, "to dance with Arnie and to be there for our children and grandchildren."

"What grandchildren?" said Arnold in surprise.

"The one on the way and those in the future!" she said knowingly.

"Oh, Arnie, Harriet is expecting, I know they haven't told us yet, but I know the signs!" and of course she was absolutely right.
"It must have been a real wrench leaving home then," said Arnold quietly.

"Yes," Penelope said, "but I did it for you!"

The most peculiar, warm, fuzzy feeling came over Arnold again and he was quite incapable of speaking, but he reached out his wing and drew his beautiful wife under it in a most possessive and protective way. Penelope seemed to be glowing all over, she was just so very happy.

"Yes," said William interrupting. "Family is very important and your children need you. They must always come first after us."

"Before we send you back, however, we have a lovely gift for you," said Mama Owl and presented them with a large yellow gift box tied with a blue ribbon. Inside the box, nestled among the tissue paper, were two pairs of shoes. Penelope's were gold and sparkly and Arnold's were white with the same gold sparkly bit around the edges.

"Come on," said William, "try them on!"

As the puffins pulled on these very beautiful shoes, something changed inside their heads. They understood who they were at last and the shoes fitted them to perfection. A new boldness and courage filled them and they knew that this mission was very important indeed.

Papa, Mama and William Owl looked on lovingly, "Oh, you are so very beautiful and special!" they hooted in unison. "We are so very pleased with you".

CHAPTER 20

THE CAVE

Meanwhile, back at the waterside, a storm was brewing and the once calm pond had become like a rough sea. The three young puffins were sitting quietly wondering what they were supposed to do now. William had told them not to do anything unless he or his friends told them to. Peter didn't seem to be his usual impatient self, and was reluctant to do anything. Rudolph and Tobias were getting very frustrated, however, and tried to persuade Peter to dive into the rough pond with his sword, but Peter would not budge, he seemed to be anchored to the floor all of a sudden. Rudy and Toby were not natural leaders and seemed unwilling to step out without Peter. So, they waited and waited, sheltering from the storm in a little cave.

Funny things began to happen inside that cave. Waves of love and compassion would flood over them followed immediately by great sobs pushing up from the depths of themselves, a depth that they never even realised existed. These sobs would tear through their little bodies leaving them quite spent and exhausted. After a brief respite, the laughter would begin, everything seemed incredibly funny and became more and more hilarious as the day wore on. This continued for some days, grief and uncontrolled sobbing followed by the most joyous laughter, after which they would fall asleep utterly exhausted.

One morning, they woke to calmness and stillness, the storm seemed to have passed. They suddenly felt very hungry indeed and realised that they hadn't eaten for days, not since they entered that cave.

"How odd," said Peter, "I can't normally go for more than a few hours without food!"

They decided to venture outside, and there an amazing sight greeted them at the pond. It was full of every sort of wildlife imaginable, surrounded by a pink glow of flamingos encircling the whole pool.

A little frog hopped over to them and introduced herself as Frieda and invited them to join in the party. A great feast was going on and everyone seemed to be celebrating and to be very excited to meet them. After they had eaten and drunk their fill, they asked Frieda what they were celebrating.

"Why, you of course," she said and jumped into the water and disappeared leaving only the ripples in the water showing where she had been.

"How very odd!" said Rudy, and the other two agreed.

"Excuse me, young sirs," interrupted a very tall flamingo. "Will you follow me please?"

He saw the three puffins looking rather reluctant and continued, "Daniel is waiting for you!"

"Oh," they cried, relief flooding through them and they followed the flamingo round to a deeper part of the pond. A splash and a flounce of blue tail announced Daniel's arrival.

"Well, welcome, you three have been very busy haven't you? We can't thank you enough!" he said and dived back under the water and summersaulted up into the air again. Peter, Rudy and Toby needed no further invitation and in they went after him.

As they travelled down deeper under the water, something strange began to happen around their necks and they seemed to be able to breathe underwater. They had bright new breathing tubes which were plugged straight into William. Their eyes also glazed over with a protective film and they were able to keep their eyes open. They had never realised what a beautiful world there was waiting for them under the water. They saw the most stunning coral reefs and yet all the fish seemed to keep their distance!

At last, Daniel led them to a dark cave, which looked mysteriously like the one they had inhabited above ground. Outside the cave, they were met with a very strange sight. A very glum octopus was sitting plonked on the floor, his six arms and two legs seemed to be missing. He was crying inconsolably, "Oh, woe is me, woe is me, what is to become of me!" he kept saying over and over again.

Daniel spoke, "we can't seem to get through to him at all!" He explained to the puffins that the octopus had been the jailor keeping all the prisoners captive in that cave. But a few days ago each one of his arms and legs mysteriously disappeared, one by one. He is very upset because he knows he is in deep trouble. All the prisoners have escaped and his cruel master is returning soon and Oliver is very frightened. For some reason, he thinks he is going to be killed off completely and we cannot get through to him at all!

"What can we do?" asked Peter.

"Have you brought your swords?" Daniel asked, and the three puffins nodded bravely.

"It is time to use them to bring healing and to restore his arms and legs!" the dolphin pronounced grandly.

"But we can't do that!" said Peter.

"Oh, yes you can!" Daniel continued, "only those who cut the tentacles off have the power to restore them again."
"But we didn't cut off his legs!" the puffins squeaked in utter shock.
"Oh, but you did," Daniel said, "we all saw you!"

All of a sudden, William appeared at their side.

"I had better explain," he said and led the surprised puffins into the empty cave. Inside the cave, there were chains lying on the ground and the evidence of many prisoners held captive was obvious. They saw litter and the words HELP written on the cave wall with the number of days, months and years the prisoners had been held captive.

"The escaped prisoners were all the wildlife that you saw around the pond. They were celebrating their freedom. You, Peter, Rudy and Toby, helped to set them free because while you were in that cave crying with compassion and love and asking for help to set them free, I went to work, sending out my messengers. You three really did cut off Oliver's legs, you did it through your prayers, I then strengthened you with my joy because it took so much out of you.

"So that is why we were laughing!" said the puffins, understanding coming at last.

"Now, Oliver, desperately, needs your help. You are to tell him that you love him and that I am to be his new master. Use your swords and touch him where his arms and legs used to be, and they will grow back and be better and stronger than ever before. However, you must believe that I can do this," said William seriously, "otherwise, Oliver cannot be healed!"

The puffins had no problem believing that William could do this, they had seen him full of light as the Snowy White Owl, they knew William had special powers.
"Remember, it is love that sets puffins and all the other creatures free!" said William.

Peter and the twins followed William out of the cave, then he stood to the side and waved his wing as if to say, get on with it. Peter looked a bit unsure, but he took out his sword and the twins copied him. Oliver saw them and went into a renewed frenzy of wailing, he was terrified of them, it seemed! Oliver's fear emboldened Peter and he took his sword and hid it behind his back.

69

Oliver calmed down a bit and Peter began to sing to him. It was the most amazing love song that came out of nowhere. Peter was incredibly impressed with himself, but he was not so silly as to think it was him, he knew William was behind it all. Oliver had calmed right down, and Peter told him how much the three puffins loved him and that they had a friend who was also their master. Peter told Oliver that he was special and very loved, and this seemed to send poor Oliver into a wave of uncontrollable sobbing once more. Snot seemed to pour out from all his pores and things got somewhat messy for a while.

Buckets appeared out of thin air and the biggest clean up job that the puffins had ever witnessed began to take place with little goldfish appearing everywhere. As the goldfish worked, they danced and sang in a most beautiful way, so much so that it brought tears to the puffin's eyes.

"Now!" said William, pointing to the puffin's swords, and while Oliver was distracted by the singing goldfish, the three puffins pointed their swords where Oliver's arms and legs used to be. There was an almighty shout and Oliver jumped up out of the water in a dizzying display of dancing legs. Suddenly, Oliver was hugging the three puffins all at the same time with his brand new arms.

There was a commanding hoot, and everyone knew it was time to give Oliver and William some privacy, and off they went travelling up to the surface in double quick time.

CHAPTER 21

EAGLE ROCK

Sven and Hanne were beside themselves with excitement after hearing that Archibald and Matilda were going to stay in Sweden. Interestingly, there was a small colony not far from them which had been struggling for some time. Eagle Rock was not too far away, but despite their best efforts to help, it was too far to lead them from such a distance. Many of the families had been in that area for a very long time and they seemed very reluctant to move. The old leaders had had to leave suddenly after one of them had a breakdown, they needed time out to rest and heal. Would Archie and Matilda like to take a look at it and see if it would suit them? they asked.

"How exciting?" exclaimed Matilda and suddenly she started to remember her dream.

"Well, there is no time like the present," said Sven and he waved his wing and told them to follow him. So off they went flying side by side across the snow covered landscape.

After they had been flying for quite some time, Sven began to point with his wing and began his descent, the other puffins followed right behind. As they came into land, Matilda gasped out loud, she had seen this place before, in her dream!

There was a very large rock which jutted outwards over the sea. It was part of some cliffs which formed themselves into the many islands that made up this part of the coastline. The rock looked just like the head of a great eagle and seemed to hover over and protect the island underneath.

We are home!" Matilda said out loud and Archie knew she was right.

Puffins began to gather together under Eagle Rock, they came from every direction as if drawn by some invisible force. Sven and Hanne introduced them to Archibald and Matilda.

"Oh, thank you for coming so promptly, we have been expecting you," said a tiny little puffin in front of them.

72

"William promised that he would send leaders soon and here you both are. How wonderful to meet you, I am Valentina," and she held out her wing in a greeting.

Archie and Matilda felt a little overcome, but suddenly they both heard William's hoot in their ears saying, "You can do this, you were born for this. Trust me and I will help you."

Courage and excitement began to build in Archie and Matilda as they were shown their new nesting place. It was just perfect! A celebration feast was being prepared and the most delicious fish began to appear in front of them.

"How?" began Archie seeing the frozen lake on the island.

A tall, gangly puffin stood to attention, his name was Henry and he would be very important moving forward. He was a mine of information and showed Archie the hole cut through the ice. The hole began to get bigger and bigger as more fish were brought out by the many puffins surrounding it. There was a large crack and the ice began to break off into chunks. The thaw had begun and the puffins started to clap their wings in glee.

Later on that night when all the festivities had ended, Archie and Matilda lay holding one another in their new nesting place overlooking the sea. "Apparently this area is full of yachts in the summer!" said Matilda.
"Well, what an adventure!" said Archie," and it has only just begun!" and off they went to sleep happily, feeling protected and guarded by the Eagle Rock towering overhead and the reassuring hoots of the owls in the distance.

CHAPTER 22
PUFFIN ISLAND

Over the next few days, the remaining puffins drifted back home to Puffin Island. Big changes were waiting for them on their return. The three young puffins were going to enrol in William's new school and they were rather surprised to find that Arnold and Penelope were going to be their teachers. Peter began to groan inwardly when William appeared at his side.

"Peter, just as you have been changed by your journey, so have your mother and father. They have a lot to teach you, especially about dancing!"

"Dancing?" Peter squawked in dismay, and William smiled as he knew what a long way Peter had to travel before he would realise his dream of becoming a leader himself.

"However, young Peter, you will be able to teach them everything that you, Rudy and Toby have learnt. The great thing about my new school is that everyone will help one another."

"Oh cool!" Peter exclaimed with excitement.

"Oh and by the way, grumpy Graham wants to be your friend, and I have plans for you two together."

Peter was appalled, but did his best to hide his feelings of aversion and promised William that he would try, crossing his wings behind his back.

William chuckled and shouted out as he flew off, "I can see in front of you and behind, I can see every side of you, inside as well as out. I know you through and through, you cannot hide anything from me," and with that, William soared into the sky and the whole island lit up in the most extraordinary golden glow.

Inexplicably, all Peter was able to do was dance, dance like he had never danced before, whirling and twirling until he was quite dizzy.

Then he sat down next to grumpy Graham and shared his supper with him.

THE END

ABOUT THE AUTHOR

Mandy has a desire for people to discover the person of Jesus instead of religion. Jesus loves us so much that he was willing to die for us so that all our mistakes could be forgiven and taken away, it's as if we never did anything wrong at all. He has an amazing Father who loves us just as we are and they just want us to believe in them and trust them and ask them into our hearts. The amazing thing is, that when we do, they send the Holy Spirit to come into us and change us from the inside out. Then the adventure begins. What have you got to lose? If you are not sure that God exists, ask him to show you and he will.

May you, dear reader, have your own adventure just like Archie and his family did.

Mandy and her husband Andrew have a website where you can find more stories, poems, songs and teaching. It is a place where people can come together to share and learn from one another in creative ways.

Website address is: www.comeawaywithme.org

77

Lightning Source UK Ltd.
Milton Keynes UK
UKHW051909260321
381043UK00006B/148